MAHAB:
HOW IT ALL BEGAN

VEDA VYASA

www.realreads.co.uk

Retold by Prema Jayakumar
Illustrated by K. R. Raji

Published by Real Reads Ltd
Stroud, Gloucestershire, UK
www.realreads.co.uk

Text copyright © DC Books, 2010
Illustrations copyright © DC Books, 2010
Published in conjunction with DC Books, Kottayam, Kerala, India

First published in 2011

ISBN 978-1-906230-31-9

Printed in Malta by Gutenberg Press Ltd
Typeset by DC Books, Kottayam, Kerala, India

CONTENTS

The Characters   4

Mahabharata
How it all began   7

Taking things further   55

THE CHARACTERS

Bhishma

Born Devavrata, Bhishma is heir to the kingdom of Bharata, but gives up his right to the throne for his father's sake. Can he prevent the kingdom from being destroyed?

Dhritarashtra

Bhishma's eldest nephew, Dhritarashtra was born blind, so his younger brother, Pandu, rules the land. Can he secure the country for his sons, the Kauravas?

Duryodhana

Dhritarashtra's firstborn son, Duryodhana is the eldest Kaurava. He does not see why his cousins the Pandavas should ever rule the country, just because their father Pandu did.

Kunti

A strong woman and Pandu's widow, Kunti has to bring up five fatherless children on her own. Will she see them claim their inheritance?

The Pandavas

Pandu's sons, the Pandava brothers must guard themselves against the treachery of their cousins, the Kauravas.

Draupadi

Beautiful Draupadi marries the Pandava prince, Arjuna, but becomes the wife of his four brothers as well. Can they protect her honour?

THE FAMILY TREE OF THE KURU RACE

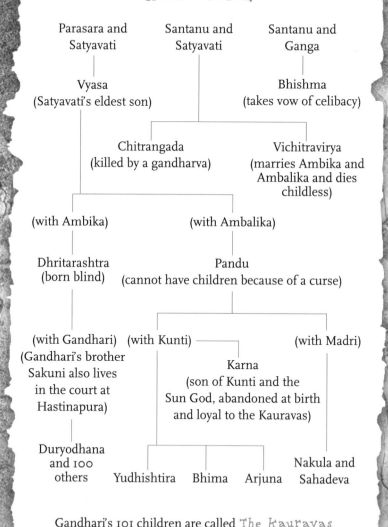

Parasara and Satyavati
|
Vyasa (Satyavati's eldest son)

Santanu and Satyavati

Santanu and Ganga
|
Bhishma (takes vow of celibacy)

Chitrangada (killed by a gandharva)

Vichitravirya (marries Ambika and Ambalika and dies childless)

(with Ambika)

(with Ambalika)

Dhritarashtra (born blind)

Pandu (cannot have children because of a curse)

(with Gandhari) (Gandhari's brother Sakuni also lives in the court at Hastinapura)

(with Kunti)

(with Madri)

Karna (son of Kunti and the Sun God, abandoned at birth and loyal to the Kauravas)

Duryodhana and 100 others

Yudhishtira   Bhima   Arjuna

Nakula and Sahadeva

Gandhari's 101 children are called The Kauravas
Kunti's and Madri's 5 children are called The Pandavas

MAHABHARATA
HOW IT ALL BEGAN

In the north of India lay the splendid city of Hastinapura, capital of the kingdom of Bharata. For centuries it had been ruled by lofty rulers of the Kuru race, but it was under King Santanu that the downfall of this glorious race – and our story – begins.

King Santanu was hunting on the banks of the River Ganga when he spied a beautiful young woman. Mesmerised by her beauty, he approached her and said, 'I am Santanu, the king of Bharata. I have fallen in love with you. Will you marry me?'

The young woman demurred. 'Oh king,' she said, 'I can only marry someone who will agree to let me live according to my wishes.' After much persuasion she finally agreed. But she warned Santanu, 'If you ever question anything that I do, I shall leave you.'

The king was willing to agree to anything to win her as his wife. They lived happily for a while, and in due course a son was born to them. But to King Santanu's horror, the queen took the baby to the banks of the Ganga and threw him into the river. Though very upset, the king remembered his promise and suffered in silence.

The same fiendish act was repeated after the birth of six more sons. Finally, when the eighth son was born, the king could bear it no longer, and stopped his queen before she could throw the baby into the river.

Tearfully she told him, 'I am Goddess Ganga, the deity of the river. I am compelled to do this to rid our sons of a curse from their previous life. As you have broken your word, I must now leave you. I am taking our son away with me. He will return to you when he has completed his education.'

Several years later the boy, who was named

Devavrata, returned to his father's court, well-versed in the arts of peace and war.

One day, on a visit to the forest, King Santanu was attracted by a wonderful smell of lotus flowers. He traced the scent to its source – a beautiful young woman who was ferrying people across the river. Forgetful of his vanished wife, Santanu fell in love with her.

'Maiden,' said the king, 'I am the king of Bharata, Santanu by name. Please be my wife and the queen of Bharata.' The young woman, whose name was Satyavati, told him to talk to her father, king of the fishermen.

Satyavati's father did not welcome the proposal. 'It is a great honour that you offer my daughter, but I have sworn that she must marry a man who can make her son a king. You already have a son who will inherit your throne.'

Disappointed, Santanu went back to his court, haunted by the sweet perfume of lotus flowers. Devavrata, now a young man, noticed that his father was unhappy. When he found out about Satyavati he went to the fisher king and asked him to let Satyavati be his father's queen.

The fisher king was adamant, 'I have sworn that my daughter's son will be a king, and that cannot happen if she marries your father Santanu. You are the firstborn, and thus heir to Bharata.'

Devavrata reassured Satyavati's father. 'If that is all that troubles you, I swear I will renounce my right to the throne. The sons born to my father and Satyavati shall inherit the kingdom.'

The fisher king was still unconvinced. 'I see you are sincere in your oath, but your children may not see it in the same light. They will want what they see as their rightful

inheritance.' Devavrata once again swore, with
the elements and gods as witnesses to his oath,
'I shall not marry or have children. There will
be no one to dispute the right to the throne.'

The elements and gods were stunned by
the vehemence of Devavrata's promise. From
that day Devavrata was known as Bhishma –
the one who took the terrible oath.

So Santanu married Satyavati, and they lived happily for several years. Two sons were born to them, Chitrangada and Vichitravirya. The boys' half-brother Bhishma supervised their education, and saw to it that they were well-versed in kingly skills. Chitrangada met with an untimely death and so, when Santanu died, Vichitravirya inherited the kingdom of Bharata.

It was time for the young king Vichitravirya to get married. Bhishma heard that the king of Kasi was holding a swayamvara for his three daughters, where each would choose her own husband from the young men visiting the court. An old rivalry between the kingdoms of Kasi and Bharata meant that Vichitravirya was not invited, so Bhishma decided to attend instead. There was much laughter and many sly comments about such a confirmed bachelor attending the swayamvara.

The three beautiful princesses – Amba, Ambika and Ambalika – appeared at the entrance of the hall. Before anyone had a chance to stop him, Bhishma snatched all three of them up, bundled them into his chariot, and set out for Hastinapura. Though the kings who had come for the swayamvara gave chase, they failed to stop Bhishma's chariot.

When they reached Hastinapura, Amba told Bhishma that she was in love with another king. Bhishma agreed to set her free, but her proud lover would not accept her back. Amba then asked Bhishma to marry her. When Bhishma explained that he had taken a vow not to marry, Amba became very distraught. Amba died soon

afterwards, vowing revenge on Bhishma.

Both Ambika and Ambalika were married to king Vichitravirya, but he did not live long enough to bear any children. Bharata was now without a king.

Satyavati called her stepson Bhishma to her, and told him, 'You took a terrible oath so that I could marry your father and my sons would be kings. They are now dead, so the reason for your oath no longer exists. It is your duty to take over the kingdom, to marry and beget heirs.'

But Bhishma was adamant. 'Mother, I took the oath and I shall not deviate from it. We must find some other way to get an heir to protect the land.' Satyavati had to give in.

She told Bhishma, 'Years before I met your father, the sage Parasara blessed me with a son, the wise Vyasa. Vyasa left me, yet promised he would return whenever I needed him. I now have no choice but to call upon him.'

True to his promise, Vyasa appeared in an instant. His mother told him, 'It is stated in the sastras, the sacred scriptures, that it is a man's duty to marry his brother's widows for the sake of heirs. Ambika and Ambalika have been left widows by your half-brother, and you shall now marry them, so that they may have children to continue the lineage of this kingdom.'

So Vyasa married Ambika. On their wedding night Ambika was repulsed by this uncouth sage, and closed her eyes. As a result her son Dhritarashtra was born blind, and therefore unable to be king. At Satyavati's request, Vyasa also married Ambalika. Ambalika turned pale when Vyasa came near her, and her son Pandu was born unnaturally pale.

Ambika's maid served Vyasa with great respect, and Vyasa blessed her with a son. This boy was named Vidura, and as he grew up he became as wise as his father Vyasa.

The boys Dhritarashtra and Pandu were taught the arts of war and statecraft, but Dhritarashtra's blindness meant he could not take part in many physical arts and games. It also barred him from becoming king, even though he was the elder and rightful heir to the throne.

So in due course Pandu became king and
took two princesses, Kunti and Madri, to be
his wives. Dhritarashtra married Gandhari,
a princess named after her homeland, the
northern kingdom of Gandhara. On learning
that her husband had been born blind,
Gandhari declared that she did not want to
experience any pleasure that was denied to her
husband. She bound her eyes with a piece of

cloth and accepted voluntary blindness for the rest of her married life. Gandhari's brother Sakuni accompanied her to the court of Hastinapura, and stayed on to help her.

One day Kunti found her husband Pandu in a pensive mood. 'What is it that troubles you so, my lord?' she asked.

'I have been cursed,' he told her, 'and cannot touch a woman. We cannot have children.' Pandu explained that he had killed a deer while out hunting. The deer was a sage in disguise who had put a curse on Pandu, saying that if Pandu ever touched a woman again he would die.

Kunti thought for a while, then said to Pandu, 'When I was young, a learned sage instructed me in a very special mantra, and gave me a boon that any god I invoke with that mantra will bless me with a son. We can use the mantra to have children.' Pandu was very relieved.

But Kunti had a dark secret. She did not tell Pandu that when she was a young girl in her father's palace, she had been curious and had tried out the mantra. She had invoked the sun god, who had blessed her with a son. The boy had been born, bright as the sun, wearing golden earrings and bright armour. Fearing disgrace, she had put the child in a casket and sent him floating down the river that flowed by the palace. A charioteer and his wife had found the boy, and raised him as their own.

With Pandu's permission, Kunti first invoked Dharmaraja, the god of righteousness. He appeared before Kunti and declared, 'I bless you with a son. Name him Yudhishtira. He will be the most virtuous of men.'

Kunti next invoked Vayu, the powerful wind god, and a strong son was born whom they named Bhima.

Then the king of gods, Indra, appeared before Kunti in all his celestial beauty. He blessed her. 'You will have a son invincible in war. Call him Arjuna.'

Then Kunti taught Madri the sage's mantra, so Madri too would not be childless. Madri invoked the twin gods of medicine, and had twin boys who were named Nakula and Sahadeva.

The five sons of Pandu became known as the Pandavas, after their father.

Soon after the birth of his five sons, the curse on Pandu killed him. Kunti, though she grieved for Pandu, remained strong, but Madri was unable to bear Pandu's passing and gave up her life. Kunti was left looking after all five of the Pandavas.

After Pandu's death, his elder brother Dhritarashtra ruled as regent. Gandhari was blessed by the sage Vasishta, who told her she would be the mother of a hundred sons. Though Gandhari conceived, no babies arrived, and she grew increasingly doubtful about Vasishta's boon.

When she heard that Kunti was a mother while she still had no offspring, Gandhari flew into a fit of rage. She beat on her stomach, which sent her into labour, but what she delivered was just a lifeless piece of flesh.

Dhritarashtra and Gandhari were distraught, but Vasishta assured them that his boon was not in vain. They divided the flesh into a hundred and one pieces and put each carefully into a jar; after a while one hundred boys and one girl were born. The eldest son they named Duryodhana.

The children of Dhritarashtra and Gandhari became known as the Kauravas, because Dhritarashtra was the eldest living descendant of the noble Kuru race.

The five Pandavas and the many Kauravas all grew up in the palace at Hastinapura, where Dhritarashtra acted as regent now that Pandu was dead. There was always intense rivalry between the two sets of cousins. Dhritarashtra resented the fact that his blindness prevented him from being the king, though he had been the firstborn, and his resentment seeped into the minds of his children.

There were only five Pandavas, but one of them was the magnificently strong Bhima, son of the wind god. In any fight, the cousins were well matched because the strength of numbers was more than set off by the great strength of Bhima. When provoked, he would pummel his cousins and immerse them in the river, and make them regret they had started the fight.

Duryodhana and his brothers could not bear the humiliation of losing out to the small band of Pandavas. One day, Duryodhana called his brothers together. 'We are always losing the fights we have with our cousins because Bhima is so strong. If he was not with them, the rest of the Pandavas would never be able to hold their own against us. It is always Bhima who gets the better of us. We need to get rid of him.'

Bhima was huge, and had an appetite to match. One day after the cousins had been camping by the river, the Kauravas put poison in Bhima's food. Bhima went into a swoon, and the Kauravas dragged him into the river, weighting him with stones so that he would drown.

Unfortunately for the Kauravas, the weight of the stones took Bhima straight to the netherworld where the king of serpents had his court. The snakes bit Bhima, but the snake venom acted as an antidote to the poison, and Bhima revived. The king of serpents was so impressed by this human being who did not die from snake venom that he gave him the strength of ten thousand elephants as a boon.

When Bhima came back out of the river, much stronger and angrier than ever, the Kauravas had even more of a problem to deal with.

The children were growing up, and needed to be trained in the use of weapons. Bhishma went in search of a good teacher. One day, as the boys were playing together in the palace grounds, their ball fell into a disused well. The well was too deep for any of them to go down safely. As they stood around wondering what to do, they heard a voice. 'Have you lost something in the well?' They turned and saw a weary-looking bearded brahmin scholar.

They told the brahmin about the lost ball, and he replied, 'I'll get the ball out for you. What will you give me in return?' The boys assured him that if he was successful they would take him to Bhishma, the man they called grandfather, who would reward him.

The brahmin plucked a blade of grass from the ground, murmured something, and threw it into the well. Then he plucked another, and another, throwing each in turn into the well. The boys were puzzled, but after a while they could see the blades of grass appearing over the top of the well – when they looked more carefully they saw that each blade had fallen directly on top of the previous one, forming a green rope. The end of the rope was now within reach, and the brahmin pulled the ball out.

Full of admiration, the boys took the brahmin to their grandfather. 'I am Drona,' the brahmin told Bhishma, 'and I come in search of employment.' Bhishma was very pleased. Though he had been born into the peace-loving caste of brahmins, Drona had a reputation as a peerless exponent in the art of war. Bhishma knew that he could not find a better teacher for his wards. So Drona came to live in Hastinapura, with his wife and son Aswathama, and the education of the princes started.

Drona was a good teacher and trained the boys well in the use of a range of weapons. Bhima and Duryodhana were fond of the mace, a heavy club, while Arjuna and Aswathama excelled in archery. When the boys were accomplished in the martial skills, Drona gave them an archery test, the bow and arrow being the weapon most often used by royal warriors.

Drona placed a bird made of mud on the branch of a tree and asked each of the boys to take an arrow and aim it at the bird.

He started with Yudhishtira, Pandu's eldest son. As Yudhishtira took aim, Drona asked, 'What do you see? Do you see the bird?'

Yudhishtira replied, 'I see the bird.'

'Is that all you see?'

'I see the tree and the bird. I see you. I see my brothers.'

Drona went through the same exercise with the other brothers, who all replied much as Yudhishtira had. Finally, Arjuna took up his bow. Drona repeated his question.

'Sir, I see only the bird,' said Arjuna.

'Can you see the whole bird?'

'I see only the bird's neck.'

Drona instructed Arjuna to fire the arrow, which pierced the neck of the mud-bird.

'You must always concentrate on the matter in hand,' explained Drona. 'Only that, nothing else.'

'The princes have now mastered their weapons,' Drona told Dhritarashtra and Bhishma at court the next day, 'It is time for them to show their skills to you and the world. Let us have a graduation ceremony and celebrate with a feast.'

Dhritarashtra, Bhishma, the queens Gandhari and Kunti, and many others all came to watch and applaud. The princes put on a wonderful show, creating fire and wind and rain with their arrows. Floods were created and dried up again. Maces flashed so fast that the eye could not follow them. In their exhibition match Duryodhana and Bhima had to be separated by Drona before they could really harm each other.

There was, however, no shadow of a doubt that Arjuna was the star of the show, his bow and arrows performing miraculous deeds.

The princes completed the demonstration
of their skills. Drona now called for anyone
from the audience who wanted to demonstrate
their own prowess.

A handsome young man entered the arena.
Though he was dressed in ordinary clothes

rather than royal attire, none could miss his brilliant earrings and his shimmering gold armour. Who was this mysterious stranger who at times surpassed even Arjuna?

Having proven his excellence in weaponry to the assembled company, he proclaimed, 'Arjuna, I challenge you to single combat.'

The crowd sat in stunned silence. Who would dare challenge the royal prince?

'Who are you?' asked Drona. 'What is your lineage? Are you aware that only a royal warrior can challenge another to single combat?'

His head held high, the young man replied, 'I am Karna, the son of a charioteer.' He knew that his lineage made the challenge impossible.

Powerless to defend himself against the taunting remarks of the Pandavas about his lineage, Karna was about to leave the arena.

Suddenly a voice bellowed from the royal stand, 'A king can be born, or can become one by conquest, or can be given land to rule and thus become a king. I, Duryodhana, hereby make Karna the king of Angarajya.'

Karna wept tears of gratitude. 'I swear eternal fealty to Prince Duryodhana, who has saved my honour.'

The elders ruled that the graduation ceremony was a show of individual skill, rather than a competition, so Karna and Arjuna did not face one another in combat that day. Duryodhana, however, knew that he had earned a mighty and faithful ally.

In all the noise and confusion no one noticed that Kunti had fainted. She alone recognised Karna, her firstborn, the son she had forsaken in the name of honour.

You will remember that Dhritarashtra's blindness had barred him from becoming king, even though he was the elder son. Pandu had reigned instead and, after he died, Dhritarashtra acted as regent with the wise Bhishma and Vidura as his advisors. But now Pandu's sons were young men, and discussions started in the court about returning the throne to its true line, making Yudhishtira, Pandu's eldest son, the new king.

Dhritarashtra's son Duryodhana could not bear this. The throne that he thought he should inherit from his father was about to pass to the cousins he disliked so heartily. 'If my father had not been blind I would have been king!' he told himself. However, the Pandavas were strong, and Duryodhana feared that he would be unable to defeat them and win the throne. Acting on his uncle Sakuni's advice, he decided that the Pandavas had to be killed.

Duryodhana went to his father and said, 'Father, there is talk in the court about handing over the kingdom to the Pandavas. You should have been king, being the eldest. The throne was given to Pandu unfairly. After you, it should pass to me, not to the sons of Pandu. We must get rid of the Pandavas before they become more powerful, and we must do it away from the eyes of the subjects, who are too fond of them. All I want you to do is send them to see the festival in Varanavata. I shall take care of everything else.'

Dhritarashtra demurred and felt he should ask more about the plan. But he too wanted the kingdom to be his, and to pass it on to his eldest son. So he did not ask any more questions, and agreed to persuade the Pandavas to go to the festival.

Dhritarashtra sent for Yudhishtira and told him, 'Now that you have completed your education, it is time for you to see a little of the world. The festival in Varanavata is very famous, and the king there has been inviting us to visit his country for some time. Why don't you take your mother and brothers to see the festivities?'

Yudhishtira knew that there was something wrong when his uncle was so insistent on his visiting a place so far away from Hastinapura. However, he could not disobey the king, and he asked his mother and brothers to get ready for the journey. He told them that the king had made arrangements for their stay there.

In the meantime, Duryodhana's uncle Sakuni had called an expert builder who he knew was loyal. He said, 'You must go to Varanavata and build a house there. Tell the people there that the Pandavas' stay there should be memorable. The house should be beautiful and have all possible luxuries, but make sure that you use lac and other materials that will catch fire easily.'

The Pandavas bade farewell to the elders.
When they went to say goodbye to their
uncle, Vidura, he murmured cryptically to
Yudhishtira, 'A forest fire does not kill the rat
that shelters in a hole, or a porcupine that
burrows in the earth. The stars give the wise
man his bearings.' Yudhishtira realised that
he was being warned of attack by fire, and was
being given advice about how to escape it.

When the Pandavas reached Varanavata, they
were escorted to the beautiful house that
had been built for them. Yudhishtira told his
mother and Bhima, 'The walls of this luxurious
house are made of combustible materials. I
have been warned by Vidura to fear fire. We
must be vigilant.'

Vidura had also made his own special
arrangements. He sent an expert miner who,
from the first night onwards, built a secret

tunnel, which eventually reached from the house out beyond the ramparts of the city. Each night, one of the Pandavas stayed awake in case of a sudden attack. By day, the family acted like carefree visitors; they went hunting in the forest and took part in the festivities. But the visits to the forest had an ulterior motive. They were also making themselves familiar with the paths of the forest.

Late one night, their arrangements were complete. Bhima ushered his mother and brothers into the tunnel, then went back to set fire to the house of lac. The deceitful builder saw the fire, and believed that an accident had made Duryodhana's wish come true.

The people of Varanavata and Hastinapura woke up to the terrible news of the death of the Pandavas and Kunti. People congregated and murmured to one another, 'How could such a grand house catch fire so quickly? This was no accident. This was done on purpose by Duryodhana to prevent the kingdom from passing to the Pandavas.'

The king and court went into mourning, and all the rituals of death were performed. Vidura too looked sad, though he knew that the Pandavas had escaped. He shared his knowledge only with Bhishma.

Safe in the forest, the Pandavas followed the paths they had explored while out hunting. They walked for a long time, and eventually Kunti was overcome with fatigue. Bhima carried her on his shoulder, and supported his brothers as much as he could.

They crossed the River Ganga using a boat that had been provided by the far-sighted Vidura. They wandered through many miles of forest, avoiding villages and towns. Finally, they decided that they would don the disguise of brahmins and enter the next village.

A brahmin family living at the edge of the village gave the mother and five sons a place to live, and the family settled there. The five young men, still dressed as brahmins, went begging for food from house to house. Kunti cooked the food and divided it into two portions. 'Let Bhima who is forever hungry have one portion, and we can share the rest,' she said.

One day, Bhima did not go out with his brothers, but stayed with his mother. They heard the brahmin family arguing and weeping. Kunti asked them what the matter was, and if she could help in any way. The father replied, 'This is not anything you can help with. There is a demon who lives in a cave just beyond the limits of the village. He used to come into the village and kill anyone he saw. Then the village elders came to an agreement with him – we provide him with a cart filled with rice, drawn by two bullocks and

driven by a person from each house in turn. The demon eats the rice, the bullocks, and the person who drives the cart. Today, it is our turn to send someone to drive the cart.'

Kunti thought for a moment and said, 'You have treated us like family and that makes us part of your family. You have only one son, I have five. My son Bhima shall take the demon his meal.'

The brahmin family was reluctant to accept such a sacrifice, but Kunti assured them that Bhima had extraordinary powers and would come to no harm.

The next day, the villagers placed the rice in a bullock cart, and Bhima drove it to the forest where the demon lived. He drew up in front of the demon's cave.

'I have hardly had a full meal since I came to the village,' he thought. 'I will eat the rice and then tackle the demon.' But the demon had grown tired of waiting and came out of the cave. He was very hungry and very angry. He got angrier still when he saw a large human being devouring the food intended for him.

The demon threw some rocks at Bhima, but Bhima hardly noticed them. The demon threw some large trees. Bhima reluctantly abandoned the first good meal he had enjoyed in a long time and turned to attack the demon. A fierce battle ensued, and before long the demon lay dead on the ground. Bhima returned to the village to tell everyone about the battle and his victory.

The next day, Kunti called her sons to her. 'It is time for us to go away from here. The killing of this powerful demon will make people wonder about the man who killed him. They might suspect who we are. There are already rumours that the Pandavas escaped alive from the house of lac. Let us leave and go to the kingdom of Panchala.'

So they set out the next morning for Panchala. When they arrived they found the city buzzing with excitement – the princess Draupadi was soon to be married. The wedding was to be a swayamvara – the princess would choose her own bridegroom from among the princes invited.

Drupada, the king of Panchala, had heard rumours that the Pandavas had escaped the house of lac with their mother, and he hoped that Arjuna would marry his daughter. To ensure this, he had devised an ingenious test. A revolving target was placed above a small pond filled with water. A huge bow was placed beside the pond. The archer was expected to string the bow, take an arrow and shoot the target, but he was not allowed to look directly at the target, only at its reflection in the pond.

The hall was filled with kings and princes from all over the country, including Duryodhana and several of the other Kauravas. All had heard of Draupadi, the beautiful princess with the dark lustrous skin. They looked on eagerly as her brother Dhrishtadyumna led the princess into the hall.

The greatest princes in the land came forward one by one and tried to string the bow. They all found it impossible. Duryodhana and his brothers each tried and failed. Karna, Kunti's forsaken son, came forward and succeeded in stringing the bow, but his arrow missed the target.

The hall was now silent. It looked as though the princess of Panchala would remain unwed. But then a young man got up from among the brahmins and asked Dhrishtadyumna if he might try.

The youth lifted the bow, strung it, and then paused for a moment with his eyes closed. He glanced at the reflection in the pond and let fly the arrow, which pierced the target right through the middle. The hall erupted in excited arguments. The beautiful Draupadi stood up and garlanded the brahmin youth.

However, one guest watched the proceedings with calm detachment.

Krishna, Kunti's nephew and the Pandavas' cousin, was the noble and fearless king of Dwaraka. He was also the ninth avatar of Lord Vishnu, the preserver of the universe. In this avatar, Krishna's task was to steer the course of earth's destiny, ridding it of evil and reinstating a state of righteousness, or 'dharma'.

While the defeated princes protested that a brahmin had no right to take part in the competition, Krishna argued that the youth had been given permission by Dhrishtadyumna. Krishna had recognised his cousins the Pandavas among the brahmins, and he knew that the master archer was Arjuna, who was meant to marry the beautiful Draupadi.

The time came for Draupadi to leave her father's palace. The princess walked behind the brahmin youth and his brothers to the house where they were staying. Dhrishtadyumna followed secretly to see what sort of man had won his sister.

When the Pandavas came to their house, one of them called out, 'Mother, come and see what we have brought home.'

Kunti replied, 'Whatever it is, you must share it equally among the five of you.'

Kunti was shocked when she saw what it was that she had asked them to share. The brothers too looked at each other in consternation. However, they were bound by a vow of obedience to their mother, and she could not undo her words. Thus Draupadi became the wife of all five brothers.

Dhrishtadyumna was hiding behind a tree, and witnessed what had happened. He went home and told his father. 'Father, your wish has been fulfilled. The young brahmin who won Draupadi is Arjuna. He lives with his mother and four brothers in the house of a brahmin. All of them are of royal blood. The only problem is that they have decided that all five brothers will marry my sister.'

Though the king was extremely pleased with the result of his test of skill, he was upset to hear that his daughter was to have five husbands. Sage Vasishta, who was at the court, explained, 'Do not worry. Draupadi was given a boon by Lord Siva in her last life that she would have five great warriors as her husbands, and that has now come true.'

The Pandavas now had strong allies, and could finally come out of hiding. They revealed themselves to the world, and proceeded to the court at Hastinapura. They were received with great ceremony, and Dhritarashtra pretended to be very happy to see his nephews with their new wife. He realised that the Pandavas were stronger now as Draupadi's father was a powerful king and he had allies too. This was a time for reconciliation.

Dhritarashtra called Bhishma and Drona to his chamber and told them the news. Bhishma said, 'You must now give half the kingdom to Yudhishtira. You know that he is entitled to the whole kingdom, but I am sure he will be satisfied with half. You can continue to reign over your half, and pass your share on to your son.'

Drona was of the same opinion. So was the wise Vidura. Dhritarashtra knew that to do anything else would result in strife and danger, so he agreed to divide the country.

The court held a great festival to celebrate the return of the Pandavas. As the festivities drew to a close, Dhritarashtra called his nephew Yudhishtira aside and told him, 'I have decided to divide the kingdom into two. I shall continue to rule from Hastinapura. You must build a new capital in Khandava, and rule from there.'

And so the Pandavas finally had their own kingdom. They built a wonderful city in the area known as Khandava, and named it Indraprastha. It had beauties hitherto unknown to mortals.

From Indraprastha Yudhishtira ruled wisely and well, supported by the might of his brothers. But Duryodhana was still unhappy, as the question of inheritance had not been resolved.

The journey ahead would be as fickle as the roll of the dice.

TAKING THINGS FURTHER
The real read

This *Real Read* version of *Mahabharata* is
a retelling of the epic originally written in
Sanskrit by Sage Vyasa. We have divided
the book into three volumes, each dealing
with different periods in the lives of the
protagonists. This is the first volume, which
covers their birth and childhood. The second
volume is about a treacherous game of
dice and its dire consequences. The third
and final volume depicts the bloody battle
at Kurukshetra. If you would like to read a
lengthier version, there are many retellings in
English.

    Mahabharata is so full of stories that it
is sometimes said that if all the literature
in all the world's languages were lost, but
Mahabharata survived, it would be able to
replace all the lost stories.

Filling in the spaces

In compressing *Mahabharata* even into three volumes, we have had to omit a large portion of it. Some of the main stories we have had to leave out are mentioned here; the complete book is a never-ending source of stories.

• Hindus believe that Lord Vishnu will descend on earth as ten avatars to destroy evil and preserve righteousness or dharma. He has assumed nine avatars so far, Lord Rama (see the *Real Read* version of *Ramayana*) being the seventh and Lord Krishna the ninth. The tenth is yet to come. Krishna, with his wisdom and foresight, steers the course of destiny so that dharma will eventually triumph over evil.

• Ganga, the deity of the River Ganga who became the first wife of King Santanu, takes human form only to give birth to the eight sons she bears. The eight sons are all minor gods who have been cursed by sages in their previous lives.

- Princess Amba, who has been rejected both by her lover and Bhishma, vows revenge. She kills herself and is reborn as Sikhandi, whose mission is to kill Bhishma.

- Pandu, Madri and Kunti go to the forest because of the curse on Pandu, and the Pandavas are born in the forest. The Pandavas return to Hastinapura after the death of Pandu and Madri.

- After the Pandavas escape from the house of lac they wander in the forest for some time. While they are in the forest, Bhima meets and marries a demoness called Hidumbi; a son called Ghatotkacha is born to them.

- Drona refuses to teach archery to Ekalavya, a low-born tribal boy. However, Ekalavya fixes Drona in his mind as his guru and learns archery by himself, surpassing even Arjuna. Drona demands Ekalavya's thumb as an offering to his teacher, thus ensuring Ekalavya's failure and Arjuna's supremacy.

Back in time

Ramayana and *Mahabharata* are the epics which united India long ago, when the country was geographically divided into a number of small kingdoms. *Ramayana* has always been more popular for reading out loud, but *Mahabharata* raises questions on the nature of morality that remain provocative even today. It is the philosophical content of *Mahabharata* that makes it so special.

The date for the writing of the earliest version has been placed tentatively in the eighth century BCE. The author is clearly concerned with the nature of morality, and questions many of the values that were taken for granted at the time it was written. *Mahabharata* examines a wide range of moral issues. What justifies a war? When is it acceptable to take up arms, and to kill innocent people? When is deceit permissible? When does the desire for peace become cowardice?

The author of *Mahabharata* shows that there are few clearcut solutions. Fighting should be avoided, but it becomes immoral not to fight against unacceptable exploitation and tyranny. While peace is desirable, it cannot be at any cost. Any war leaves victors looking at what they have won, and losers mourning what they have lost.

None of the characters in this story is perfect, and none is so wicked that the reader can find nothing in them to admire.

Major places and festivals

- Hastinapura, in the state of Uttar Pradesh, still exists, though today it is just a small town. It is believed that Indraprastha was located near to the city of Delhi. Kurukshetra, where the final battle took place, is in Haryana.

- Kasi or Benares, on the banks of the River Ganga, is the heart of Hinduism, and its most important pilgrimage centre.

- The most important temples dedicated to Lord Krishna in North India are at Mathura, where he was born, and at Brindavan, where he grew up.

- The temple at Dwaraka, where Krishna ruled from, is in the western state of Gujarat.

- Krishna, in the form of a child, is worshipped at Guruvayur temple in the southern state of Kerala. ISKCON, which stands for International Society for Krishna Consciousness, has temples worldwide, attracting thousands of devotees.

- Janmashtami, the festival of Krishna's birth, is celebrated each year in August or September.

- Holi, the festival of colours which is celebrated in March, is associated with Krishna's childhood.

Finding out more

Books

We recommend the following books and websites to gain a greater understanding of India and *Mahabharata*.

- Anita Vachharajani and Amit Vachharajani, *Amazing India: A State-by-State Guide*, Scholastic India, 2009.

- C. Rajagopalachari, *Mahabharata*, Bhavan's Book University, 1951.

- INTACH, *Indian Culture for Everyone*, Arvind Kumar Publishers, 2007.

- Meera Uberoi, *The Mahabharata*, Penguin Books, 2005.

- Roshen Dalal, *The Puffin History of India for Children*, Puffin Books, 2002.

- *Illustrated Guide to India*, Readers Digest in association with Penguin Books, India, 2002.

Websites

- www.gutenberg.org/ebooks/7864
The Mahabharata of Krishna-Dwaipayana Vyasa, translated into English prose by Kisari Mohan Ganguli.

- www.incredibleindia.org
A comprehensive website about India's heritage and contemporary life.

- www.intach.org
Provides useful information about the history, culture, religion and society of India.

- www.iskcon.com
Information about the Krishna movement, which promotes the well-being of society by following Krishna's teachings.

- www.kamakoti.org
Provides detailed information about many aspects of Hinduism.

- www.krishna.com
Information about Krishna and ancient Hindu classics.

Food for thought

Mahabharata is a complex book, and rewards a full and careful reading. With the story having reached a natural pause at the end of the first volume, here are some ideas for further thought and discussion.

Starting points

● Which character in the story interests you the most?

● Do you feel that Dhritarashtra was justified in his grudge against the Pandavas?

● What do you think about the way in which society was structured in those days?

● Do you think the Pandavas were entitled to the entire kingdom, or just part of it?

Themes

What do you think Vyasa says about the following themes?

● dharma – leading a righteous life

● duty

● loyalty

● birth and lineage

In many ways our *Real Read* version is very far from Vyasa's original style, but can you find examples of the following in the *Real Read* version?

- disguise and deception
- sacrifice in the name of love
- the bond between brothers
- treachery

Can you write a short story using some of the same ideas?

Symbols

Writers frequently use symbols in their work to deepen the reader's emotions and understanding, and Vyasa is no exception. Think about how the symbols in this list match the action in *Mahabharata*.

- fondness for food
- the sun
- the use of codes
- weapons as symbols of superiority